Red Ned

I can read the Speed sounds.

I can read the Green words.

I can read the Red words.

I can read the story.

I can answer the questions about the story.

I can read the Speed words.

Say the Speed sounds

Consonants

*Ask your child to say the sounds (not the letter names)
clearly and quickly, in and out of order. Make sure
he or she does not add 'uh' to the end of the sounds,
e.g. ' f ' not 'fuh'.*

f	l	m	n	r	s	v	z	sh	th	ng

b	c k	d	g	h	j	p	qu	t	w	x	y	ch

Each box contains one sound.

Vowels

*Ask your child to say each vowel sound and then the word,
e.g. 'a' 'at'.*

at	hen	in	on	up

4

Read the Green words

For each word ask your child to read the separate sounds, e.g. 'r-a-n', 'th-a-t' and then blend the sounds together to make the word, e.g. 'ran', 'that'. Sometimes one sound is represented by more than one letter, e.g. 'th', 'sh', 'ck'. These are underlined.

bin   pan   bit   dust   sma<u>sh</u>

cra<u>sh</u>   <u>ch</u>op   ba<u>sh</u>   bump   sent

o<u>ff</u>   bru<u>sh</u>   <u>sh</u>ed   pi<u>ng</u>   <u>th</u>em

Read the Red words

Red words don't sound like they look. Read the word out to your child. Explain that he or she will have to stop and think about how to say the red words in the story.

made   of   s<u>ai</u>d   to   <u>the</u>   oh

no

Red Ned

Introduction
Would you like a robot to help you tidy up?
In this rhyming story Dad makes a robot to tidy
the house, but is it really a help?

Dad made Ned from
a big red bin,

a pan,
and a can,
and a bit of tin . . .

. . . zing!

"Ned can chop," Dad said.
Bash! Smash!

"Ned can mop," Dad said.
Bump, bash!

"Ned can dust," Dad said.
Smash, crash!

"Stop, stop!" Dad said.

"Stop, stop it, Ned."

Dad sent Ned off to brush the shed.

Bash.
Crash.
Smash . . .

. . . ping!

"Oh no," Dad said.
"Ned is in bits."

Dad got the bits and made them fit.

Dad made Ned from
a big red bin,

a pan,
and a can
and a bit of tin . . .

. . . zing!

Questions to talk about

Ask your child:

Page 7: What does Dad make Ned out of?

Page 12: Why does Dad tell Ned to stop?

Page 14: What do you think is happening in the shed?

Page 20: Why do you think Dad builds Ned again?

Speed words

Ask your child to read the words across the rows, down the columns and in and out of order, clearly and quickly.

tin	red	can	said	mop
smash	chop	and	them	pan
from	stop	off	shed	in
bit	big	made	fit	got